THE 75-CENT SON

JANICE GREENE

QUICKREADS

SERIES 1
- Black Widow Beauty
- Danger on Ice
- Empty Eyes
- The Experiment
- The Kula'i Street Knights
- The Mystery Quilt
- No Way to Run
- The Ritual
- **The 75-Cent Son**
- The Very Bad Dream

SERIES 2
- The Accuser
- Ben Cody's Treasure
- Blackout
- The Eye of the Hurricane
- The House on the Hill
- Look to the Light
- Ring of Fear
- The Tiger Lily Code
- Tug-of-War
- The White Room

SERIES 3
- The Bad Luck Play
- Breaking Point
- Death Grip
- Fat Boy
- No Exit
- No Place Like Home
- The Plot
- Something Dreadful Down Below
- Sounds of Terror
- The Woman Who Loved a Ghost

SERIES 4
- The Barge Ghost
- Beasts
- Blood and Basketball
- Bus 99
- The Dark Lady
- Dimes to Dollars
- Read My Lips
- Ruby's Terrible Secret
- Student Bodies
- Tough Girl

ISBN-13: 978-1-61651-186-9
ISBN-10: 1-61651-186-9
eBook: 978-1-60291-908-2

Printed in Guangzhou, China
0311/03-150-11

15 14 13 12 11   2 3 4 5 6

■ ■ ■

Javier rested his heavy hand on ChiChi's neck. He grinned sourly at the four college students gathered in front of them. "This is ChiChi," he announced. "He's also known as Mr. C-minus. Who knows? Maybe some of your learning will rub off on him."

Burning with humiliation, ChiChi quickly twisted away from his father's strong grip. He turned toward the back of the truck where the boxes were waiting. Just behind him, he heard one of the students snicker.

Hefting a box to his shoulder, ChiChi started down the ladder to the *Paloma*. She was a sleek 38-foot motorboat, a gleaming beauty that was the pride of the University's Marine Institute.

Two of the college kids followed ChiChi's example and grabbed boxes out of the truck. The other two, a round-faced girl and a tall boy with floppy blond hair, clambered down the ladder to the cabin. Their voices floated back to the others.

"Watch your head!" called the boy. "These doorways are really low!"

"Hey, Traven!" the girl yelled. "This is cool! It's got its own little kitchen!"

"It's called a *galley,* Crystal," said Traven. "And I'm not impressed unless there's a maid to go with it."

From the truck, Javier called out to ChiChi. "Be careful with those boxes, boy! This is important stuff—scientific equipment, you know!"

"Yes, sir," ChiChi grumbled.

A short, stocky girl fell in step beside ChiChi. "I'm Jenna," she said.

"Hi," said ChiChi, not looking at her.

"Hey, I'm not sure *that* box is so important," Jenna said with a grin.

ChiChi looked at the box. It was a case

of beer. He glanced down at Jenna. Her bright brown eyes were warm and friendly. He smiled in spite of his dark mood. As he stepped onto the *Paloma's* deck, he noted with pleasure the gleaming wood trim around the cabin. The boat was well cared for.

On the foredeck, Traven was wrestling with Crystal, pretending to push her overboard. She laughed shrilly, butting Traven's chest with her head.

"Come on, you slackers!" Jenna called to them. "Give Derek and me a hand!"

Shoving at each other, Traven and Crystal walked back to the truck.

With everyone helping, the truck was soon empty. Now backpacks, sleeping bags, food, and boxes labeled *Marine Lab* were jammed into the cabin. ChiChi had been hoping his dad would let him take her out of the harbor. But Javier said, "Where are your books? You brought your books—right?"

"I think you watched me pack," ChiChi said coldly.

"Don't get sarcastic with me!" said

Javier. He raised his arm and ChiChi backed up instinctively. *"Get out your books!"* he demanded.

ChiChi walked slowly to the heap of luggage piled around the dining table and found his backpack. Javier snatched it away and turned it upside down. Books and clothes tumbled onto the table. Crystal, who was in the kitchen, watched with amusement as ChiChi grabbed his underwear from the pile and shoved it back in the pack.

"All summer you have to study. *Every single day!"* said Javier. "That's the only way you'll get a good grade when you take these classes over!" He slammed a biology textbook on the table. "Here, read this one! Real science. You might learn something like these smart kids here."

ChiChi let the book fall open. It didn't matter where he started to read. Whatever it was, he wouldn't remember anyway. He was struggling through a paragraph about the parts of a plant when Derek, Crystal, and Traven came down the ladder and swarmed through the galley. Chatting with careless, confident voices, they moved past him as if he were invisible.

"Why did you want to go out with her at all, Derek? That girl's a toad," Crystal said in a mocking voice.

"That's *cold,* Crystal," Derek said. "Truth is, she looks more like a frog."

Jenna walked in from the cockpit. "Did you notice, guys?" she said. "Girls who go out with Derek are gorgeous. Girls who turn him down are ugly."

"I never said she *refused* me. Did I say that?" said Derek.

"You didn't have to," Jenna teased while the others giggled. Then the laughing college students ran up on deck—everyone but Jenna.

■ ■ ■

Jenna turned to ChiChi and started reading over his shoulder. "Are you studying this stuff for summer school?" she asked.

"No," he said, unhappily.

"I get the feeling you're not into it," she said sympathetically.

He gave her a sour smile.

"You don't like biology?" she asked.

"I hate *reading,"* said ChiChi.

"Really? Is that because you'd rather be doing something else—or is reading just hard for you?" she asked.

He searched her face. Her expression showed only curiosity and concern. He decided that he could trust her.

"The thing is that I—uh—letters get mixed up," ChiChi said quietly.

"No wonder you hate it," said Jenna. "You mean like switching *b* with *p?"*

ChiChi nodded miserably.

"So are you saying you're dyslexic? Like Tom Cruise?" said Jenna.

"Huh? Tom Cruise?" ChiChi asked in surprise.

"Right," Traven's voice boomed out from behind them. "Did you ever see that guy read anything in a movie?"

ChiChi turned. He was surprised to see

Traven rolling his long body out of a bunk bed behind them.

"Traven!" Jenna cried. "Why are you sneaking—"

But then she was interrupted by Crystal, who hollered from the deck, "ChiChi! Your dad wants you *now!*"

ChiChi charged into the cockpit. He was just in time to see a long yacht pass less than three feet from the *Paloma's* port side! A red-faced man on the yacht's deck was yelling at Javier, and Javier was screaming right back.

ChiChi's dad was sweating and swearing at the wheel, his cigarette dropping ashes on his shirt. When he spotted his son, he barked, "Take it through the harbor—I'm going below. That bunch of idiots out there can't even steer a boat!"

ChiChi took the wheel. The harbor was busy with motorboats, fishing trawlers, and beautiful sleek yachts. He guided the *Paloma* smoothly through the heavy traffic, loving the feel of her polished wooden wheel and the steady hum of her motor below.

But ChiChi's moment of peace was over all too quickly. Once out of the harbor, Javier took the wheel again. While he guided the *Paloma* to the bay beyond the new power plant, ChiChi was put to work helping the students.

"Get the raft ready," Javier ordered. "I'm taking Derek and Crystal close to the rocks. You keep the boat right here, ChiChi—and be careful. This boat's worth a lot of money!"

The inflatable raft was suspended from the davits, the long arms that stood at the back of the *Paloma*. ChiChi carefully lowered the raft to the water and brought it alongside. Derek and Crystal were waiting for it.

Crystal shouted "Me first!" and ChiChi held out his hand to help her onto the inflatable. But then Derek abruptly pushed in front of him.

"Don't fall in the drink, madam," Derek said as he took Crystal's hand.

"Hey! If I'm going in, you are, too," Crystal said as she stepped over the few inches of water that separated the *Paloma's* deck from the raft.

"Get out of the way!" Javier cried as he shouldered past ChiChi and climbed onto the raft. *"I'm* starting the motor. You go get that anchor."

"Don't you want to load the anchor first?" ChiChi said.

"Did you hear me asking for advice? Do something to earn my respect for once. *Then* I'll take your advice," Javier snapped. Then he bent over the outboard motor and pulled the cord once, twice, three times, four times. He swore.

"ChiChi!" he yelled. "Come see what's wrong with this stupid machine. Looks like somebody broke it."

ChiChi stepped onto the raft and pulled the cord on the outboard motor. It roared to life, making the raft shudder as it sent up a thin cloud of blue smoke.

"Huh," grunted Javier. "Now let's have that anchor. And be careful!"

ChiChi stepped onto the deck, hefted the

anchor, and put one foot on the vibrating raft. But the raft drifted away from the *Paloma*. The water widening between his feet, ChiChi shifted his weight back toward the deck. Javier gunned the motor, heading the raft forward much too fast. The inflatable hit the side of the *Paloma* and bounced back. ChiChi staggered and fell, whacking his shoulder against the side of the Paloma just before he splashed into the water.

The moment ChiChi went under, the shock of the frigid water hit him hard. The next second, he realized the anchor was pulling him down like a rock. There was nothing to do but let go.

He swam to the surface coughing, his hair plastered on his face. *"Estupido!"* Javier yelled. "You're going to pay for that anchor! Every last cent!"

Shaking with cold, ChiChi swam to the Paloma's ladder and hauled himself up on board.

"Are you okay?" Jenna asked. "I saw that you hit the side pretty hard."

Saying nothing, ChiChi stumbled past her, clumsy in his wet, heavy clothes. He went down to the cabin.

■ ■ ■

ChiChi changed as slowly as he dared before going on deck. Traven and Jenna were waiting for him. He didn't look at their faces, but he could hear Traven snickering.

"Hey, ChiChi, come over here and unload these boxes," Traven said.

The boxes labeled *Marine Lab* held a number of cone-shaped nets. ChiChi helped the students lower them into the water. When the nets were pulled up a minute later, ChiChi peered into them curiously. They seemed to be empty.

Jenna held one of the nets open for ChiChi. "Take a closer look," she said.

Trapped in the fine mesh were tiny, wiggling creatures. "Plankton," Jenna explained. "Lots of them are so small they can't be seen without a microscope." Then she carefully lowered the net into a jug full of sea water.

"We'll take the jugs back to the lab at school and count the plankton," Jenna went on. "Then we'll compare that number to last year's count. We want to see if waste from the new power plant is affecting the sea life in the bay."

"You *count* all these tiny things?" ChiChi asked in amazement.

Jenna laughed. "Sure do," she said. "I guess that sounds pretty tedious."

Then Traven butted in. "It's hard work if you can't count," he said. "How high can you count, Mr. C-minus?"

"Traven! Just shut *up!*" Jenna cried.

Shrugging, Traven turned back to emptying his net—but not before giving ChiChi a smarmy-sweet look that made his stomach tighten with anger.

The students worked until dark and then gathered in the cabin for dinner. When ChiChi saw Javier opening the case of beer, his heart sank. He could guess what would happen next.

Javier stationed himself in the galley,

drinking beer, rattling pans, and talking loudly to anyone who would listen. ChiChi grated cheese, heated cans of beans over the stove, and warmed tortillas in the tiny oven. He gritted his teeth, preparing for his father's ridicule.

ChiChi was setting the table when he heard Javier say, "My oldest son, he works for the city government. Very important! And my second son, he's a doctor. Went to medical school—four years! Worth a lot of money, that guy! But, unfortunately, there's my third son. He can't even make an A in school. Not one A! I figure he's worth about seventy-five cents—that's it!"

ChiChi had heard that speech so many times it seemed to be burned into his brain. He longed to leave the room—but he knew that if he did, Javier would humiliate him even more.

After three burritos, Traven pushed his plate away and started stacking empty beer cans in a tower. When they fell, he leaped up and grabbed a couple of the cone-shaped nets, which were hanging from the ceiling to dry. He held them up to his chest, dancing around the table. "I'm an exotic dancer!" he announced loudly.

"You're a goofball!" Crystal groaned. Then she snatched a net and tried to wind it around his neck.

"Hey! Stop abusing my precious body parts!" said Traven, playfully pushing her away. Then his hand struck a nearly full can of beer. It fell to the floor with a clunk, splashing in a wide circle.

"Oh, Chiii-Chiiii," Traven sang in a high, mocking voice. "It's wipe-up time!"

ChiChi stayed where he was, staring straight ahead.

"Hey guy—you deaf or something?" Traven snorted. "Clean it up!"

"ChiChi! Clean it up!" Javier roared.

Still ChiChi sat, his hands clenched.

Jenna dashed into the galley and grabbed a dishrag. She wiped up the spilled beer and then dropped the dishrag neatly over Traven's head.

Crystal and Derek laughed. Even Javier smiled. Then Traven laughed, too. He slapped at Jenna with the towel, but she jumped nimbly out of the way.

While everyone was looking at Jenna and Traven, ChiChi went up on deck. He leaned against a davit, the cold wind cooling his flushed face. He remembered his mother, patient and uncomplaining, wiping up beer his father had spilled on the table. He remembered the last time they'd visited her in the hospital. Javier Junior—polished and confident in his suit and tie—had just gotten a raise. Diego, the second son, had made her smile with stories about the hospital where he was a resident. ChiChi had had no success stories to tell her.

He heard quiet footsteps behind him. It was Jenna. She walked up quietly and sat down by his side.

"Sorry about Traven," she said. "He's like a three-year-old sometimes."

"He respects *you,* though," ChiChi said. "They all do." He wished that he had a friend like Jenna.

"Not really," Jenna said. "They're respectful because I'm the teaching assistant. They *have* to listen to me—or they won't get a good grade."

"Nah, it's more than that," ChiChi insisted. There was a sureness about Jenna, a firmness in her voice. For all of his yelling, Javier would never be respected the way Jenna was.

"Is your father always this mean to you?" Jenna asked softly.

ChiChi shrugged.

"You know what?" Jenna said. "I'm totally butting in and you can tell me to get lost if you want to—but I think you should get away from him."

"I can't," ChiChi mumbled.

"Isn't there another relative you could stay with?" said Jenna.

ChiChi thought of the spotless, modern apartments his brothers lived in. He thought of his aunts' crowded homes, boiling over with kids and dogs. No one wanted him.

He shook his head.

"You know what, ChiChi?" Jenna said. "I live in a great big house with eight roommates. One of the guys is moving out soon. Why don't you come over and check it out? The rent's cheap. Why don't you think about it? You could get another job, so you wouldn't have to work with your father anymore."

A *job?* ChiChi imagined some new boss handing him a printed page. "Just follow these instructions," he'd say. And ChiChi would stare at the hostile lines of letters and understand nothing.

"Thanks, but no. I don't think it would work," he told Jenna.

"Well, if you change your mind, give me a call," Jenna said. "I'm in the phone book. My last name's Matthison."

She got up and went to the cockpit, where she sat writing in a notebook. ChiChi wanted to talk to her, but he didn't know what to say. A few minutes later, Javier called him from the cabin.

■ ■ ■

ChiChi hurried down the steps and found Javier in the galley. His thick hands were waving in the air, and his cigarette was dangling from his lips. "The dishes!" he cried. "You leave all these dishes for *me* to do?"

"I was *going* to do them," ChiChi said to himself. Then he noticed a strong smell of gas in the room. ChiChi glanced at the stove and saw that one of the burners was turned on, but not lit. He hurried over and switched it off.

Sighing heavily, Javier put down an empty beer can and opened another. ChiChi recognized stage two of a night of drinking. Stage one, Javier was angry. Stage two, he was sorry for himself.

"Son," Javier said, "it hurts me when I see these kids here—so smart, so successful. You could be one of them! All you have to do is try!"

"I *do* try, Dad," ChiChi protested. "It's just that reading is real hard for me."

"I don't believe that!" said Javier. "You can read maps, charts—!"

It was true. For ChiChi, charts were much easier to read than paragraphs. Maybe he *wasn't* trying hard enough.

"If you could just graduate, go to college—" Javier said.

"I told you before, Dad, I don't want to go to college. I *hate* school. I just like working on boats," said ChiChi.

"Boats!" Javier spat. "A donkey can work on a boat! You can do better. That's the way it's supposed to be—the kids do something *better* than the parents—not the same back-breaking thing!"

"It's all I want! It's all I'm good for!" ChiChi cried out defensively.

"All you want is to go against me—your own father!" Javier yelled. Then he shoved ChiChi against the stove, sending a pan clattering to the floor.

Crystal came into the gallery wearing an oversized T-shirt and baggy shorts. "Hey, could you guys keep it down? You woke me up," she said.

"Sorry!" ChiChi apologized.

"I'm just *really* tired," Crystal said in a whiny, self-pitying voice. Then she walked away, almost bumping her head on the low ceiling.

Javier stared at ChiChi and sighed. "Never mind. I try my best—but I can see it's no good," he said miserably.

"Want something to eat, Dad?" ChiChi asked cautiously. He hoped that food would help to sober him up.

"The stupid stove isn't working now," Javier complained as he twisted a knob. "Go check the propane tank. We're not getting fuel."

"The tank's okay, Dad. You have to light the pilot after you turn it on," said ChiChi. "Want me to do it?"

"No, you go up on deck. See what's happening out there," said Javier.

Nothing was happening. ChiChi walked quietly onto the aft deck. Jenna and Crystal were in the berth below, probably asleep.

He sat down. From a few miles away, lights on the shore were shining softly. The stars glittered above. ChiChi took a deep, slow breath as the night air washed over his face. Again, he felt a brief moment of peace.

■ ■ ■

Then he smelled smoke and heard Javier screaming from the cabin.

ChiChi quickly guessed what happened. Javier had turned on the stove, forgotten to light it, and put his cigarette too near the escaping gas. ChiChi ran toward the cockpit just as Javier came running. The back of his shirt was in flames! ChiChi grabbed a cushion from the cockpit bench and began to beat his father's back. "Hold still!" he yelled. Javier was twisting like an eel, his eyes wide with panic.

"Hurry! *Hurry!*" he screamed.

The flaming shirt stopped burning almost immediately. Scorched bits of fabric littered the floor. Javier moaned.

ChiChi heard yells and screams from

below. *"Come on!"* he said. "They're down there!" Javier looked dazed. ChiChi knew that his father wasn't listening. "Come on!" he yelled.

Javier shook his head. "It's no use," he said numbly. ChiChi gave up. He grabbed a fire extinguisher from the cockpit wall and ran downstairs to the galley. The air grew hotter with every step. Dirty yellow smoke billowed up from the cabin, stinging his lungs.

"Crystal! Jenna!" ChiChi shouted.

"Over here!" a faint voice called out through the smoke. It was Jenna! An awful odor filled the air. To ChiChi, it smelled like something plastic was slowly melting in the heat.

The stove and counter were hidden in smoke. An orange blaze as thick as ChiChi's arm rose from the counter to the ceiling! Flames traveled along the floor and flickered up the galley walls. ChiChi pulled the pin from the fire extinguisher and sprayed a path on the floor. Then, dropping to his hands and knees below the worst of the smoke, he crawled toward the voice he'd heard.

Up ahead, ChiChi heard coughing. Then a figure came crawling through the smoke. It was Jenna, her long T-shirt pulled up over her mouth. Crystal was right behind her.

"This way!" ChiChi cried as he turned and led them to the stairs. "Come on!" he urged. Crystal doubled up at the foot of the stairs, coughing uncontrollably. ChiChi pulled and Jenna shoved until they got her up the steps to the cockpit.

From the deck, he could hear Javier yelling, "ChiChi! Get over here!"

Then there was a thump on the steps. Derek, his face black with soot, stumbled up the stairs. He collapsed on the floor, coughing and gagging.

At the same moment Javier poked his head into the cockpit. "ChiChi! Get everybody in the raft! *Hurry!*"

ChiChi ignored him. He bent over Derek. "Did you see Traven?" he asked.

"I thought he was right behind me," Derek gasped.

Thinking fast, ChiChi turned to Jenna and thrust the fire extinguisher at her. "Spray me with it!" he said.

Nodding, Jenna pulled the handle and the white foam shot out, hitting ChiChi's legs.

"Stop it! *Stop it!*" Javier yelled. He grabbed at the fire extinguisher. But ChiChi grabbed it at the same moment. Both father and son stubbornly held on, their faces separated by inches.

"You're a fool!" screamed Javier. "The propane's going to blow any minute!"

"Let go, Dad!" ChiChi cried.

"Are you *crazy?*" demanded Javier. "That college kid's gone! The boat's gone. We gotta get off!"

"It's not that bad," ChiChi insisted. "We've still got time!"

"Obey me, boy! You get in that raft, *now!*" Javier ordered.

"No!" ChiChi roared.

Javier opened and closed his mouth.

Not a word came out. Finally, ChiChi was able to wrench the fire extinguisher from his father's hands.

"Get the raft ready and tie it next to the boat," ChiChi told Javier.

Then ChiChi charged down the steps into the cabin. The entire galley was an inferno of smoke and fire. Feeling a flicker of panic, he dropped to his knees and forced himself forward. His eyes were watering so badly that he could hardly see.

Just beyond the dining area, Traven lay in a heap near the doorway. In the dim light, ChiChi saw blood on his forehead. He had a good idea about what had happened: In panic, the tall boy had run from the berth and struck his head on the low door.

ChiChi shook him hard. Traven groaned and started coughing. "Follow me!" ChiChi yelled in his ear. But Traven was only crawling, barely moving ahead. So ChiChi grabbed him under the arms and dragged him. As they passed the table, the charred legs collapsed and the tabletop fell with a crash. Then Traven's shirt caught fire! The boy screamed in pain, flailing at it weakly. ChiChi pulled off his sweatshirt and beat out the flames.

Then ChiChi started dragging Traven once more, using the dim light from the stairway as his guide. It seemed miles away. By now, his muscles ached and his chest felt scorched from the terrible heat. Traven's limp body seemed to be as heavy as stone.

At the bottom of the steps, ChiChi thought he couldn't move another inch. Then he felt arms supporting him, pulling him up. The next thing he knew he was on the deck, and Jenna and Derek were pulling him into the raft.

Someone started the outboard, and the raft pulled away quickly. They could all see flames in the cockpit now, curling around the polished steering wheel. ChiChi shut his eyes. He didn't want to watch the *Paloma* burn.

■ ■ ■

The next thing he knew, ChiChi was lying in a hospital bed. Because of all the smoke he'd inhaled, the doctor had given him some medicine to help him breathe. He'd been told he could go home soon.

Jenna poked her head in the door. Like ChiChi, she was wearing a hospital gown. "Hi," she said. "I'm not supposed to be out of bed, but I wanted to see you."

ChiChi smiled. "Come on in," he said.

"Traven has a concussion, but it's not serious," Jenna told him. "He'll stay here overnight just so they can keep an eye on him."

ChiChi felt relieved. "Is everybody else okay?" he asked.

"Everyone else can go home—thanks to you. You're a hero, ChiChi. You're the one who saved all of us," said Jenna.

ChiChi felt embarrassed. "Anybody could have done it," he mumbled.

Jenna shook her head, smiling.

ChiChi gazed at her. "I think you saved me, too," he started to explain.

But just then the door swung open and Javier walked in. He seemed startled to see Jenna standing there.

Jenna turned to ChiChi. "My folks are here, so I'll be going home soon. Goodbye, ChiChi," she said.

"Hey, I'll call you!" ChiChi said.

Jenna's eyes widened. She was surprised and pleased. *"Good!"* she said.

Javier sat down heavily on the bed. "Some people from the newspaper came for you. I told them to get lost. I mean, you're in the hospital! I guess you're some kind of big hero now," he said.

"I'll see them," ChiChi said. "If enough people hear about me, maybe one of them will give me a job."

"A job? A *boat* job?" Javier said.

ChiChi nodded.

"You're putting off going to college? You'd rather work like a donkey on some boat?" Javier cried.

"I'm *not* going to college, Dad," ChiChi said quietly.

"You think you can just go out and land yourself a job?" demanded Javier, his voice rising. "Okay, big shot—you can move out of the house then! We'll see how long you last out there. Ha! I bet you'll be back home in a week!"

Javier got up and paced back and forth across the room. ChiChi felt sad as he studied the stubborn old man. He knew that—in his own twisted way—his father loved him. And it would hurt ChiChi to leave. But enough was enough. It was time to take control of his own life. Going out on his own would be the best thing he'd ever done.

Javier turned to his son, an impatient look on his face. "Listen to me, ChiChi—" he started to say.

"Dad—my name is Chicharron," the young man interrupted. "You can call me that from now on."

After-Reading Wrap-Up

1. When ChiChi visited his mother in the hospital, why did he feel especially bad?

2. ChiChi felt that "going out on his own would be the best thing he'd ever done." Why did he feel that way?

3. What are Javier's bad points? What qualities kept him from being a hateful character?

4. How do you think Javier felt about himself?

5. During and after the fire, ChiChi is a more active character than he was earlier in the story. What did you think of ChiChi before the fire took place? What did you think of him afterward? Explain.

6. When ChiChi finally stands up to Javier, what is the single word he says?